I Didn't Do It!

Sue Graves

Illustrated by
Desideria Guicciardini

free spirit
PUBLISHING®

Poppy didn't always tell the truth at home.

"I didn't do it!" said Poppy.

Sometimes Poppy didn't tell the truth at school either. On Monday, she broke a window during morning recess.

"I didn't do it!" said Poppy.
She said that **Joe** broke the window.

Miss Plum was mad at Joe. She said he had to stay in for the rest of recess.

Joe was mad that Poppy didn't

Then Poppy spilled water over Eva's painting. Eva was upset.

Poppy said that **Lucy had done it.** Lucy was mad that Poppy didn't tell the truth.

Later on, Lucy forgot to turn off the faucet in the bathroom. Water splashed all over the floor.

Lucy said Poppy had done it.

Miss Plum said Poppy was very careless.

Poppy was mad that Lucy didn't tell the truth.

"Now you know how **we** feel when **you** tell a fib!" said Lucy.

Everyone was mad at Poppy for not telling the truth. At lunchtime, nobody wanted to play with her.

Poppy felt sad.

Poppy **felt bad** for not telling the truth.
She went to see Miss Plum.
She told her what she had done.

Miss Plum said everyone does something wrong sometimes. She said it was always **better to tell the truth.**

Miss Plum said that Poppy could make things better. Poppy nodded.

She felt sorry for lying
and making her friends angry.
Poppy told everyone, **"I'm sorry."**

Then Poppy helped Mr. Brown mend the broken window. Mr. Brown was pleased.

She helped Eva paint a new picture.
Miss Plum put it up on the wall.
Eva was pleased.

Then Poppy and Lucy promised Miss Plum to help clean the bathroom for a **whole week!**

Soon it was afternoon recess.
Everyone went outside to play.

And this time

everyone wanted to play with Poppy!

Can you tell the story of what happens when Anna knocks over the flowerpot and doesn't tell the truth?

How do you think Anna's little sister felt when Mom thought *she* kicked over the pot? Should Anna tell the truth? Why?

A note about sharing this book

The **Our Emotions and Behavior** series has been developed to provide a starting point for further discussion about children's feelings and behavior, in relation both to themselves and to other people.

I Didn't Do It!
This story explores in a reassuring way why it is important to tell the truth and the consequences that can follow when someone is not truthful.

The book aims to encourage children to have a developing awareness of behavioral expectations in different settings. It also invites children to begin to consider the consequences of their words and actions for themselves and others.

Picture story
The picture story on pages 22 and 23 provides an opportunity for speaking and listening. Children are encouraged to tell the story illustrated in the panels: Anna doesn't admit to Mom that she knocked over the flowerpot, and instead accuses her younger sister. Her sister is angry and hurt and doesn't want to play with Anna anymore. Anna realizes she has done wrong and apologizes to Mom and to her sister. She then makes things right by re-potting the plant. Her little sister is eager to play with her again, and Anna learns that it is better to tell the truth after all.

How to use the book
The book is designed for adults to share with either an individual child or a group of children, and as a starting point for discussion.

The book also provides visual support and repeated words and phrases to build confidence in children who are starting to read on their own.

Before reading the story
Choose a time to read when you and the children are relaxed and have time to share the story.

Spend time looking at the illustrations and discussing what the book may be about before reading it together.

After reading, talk about the book with the children

- What was the story about? Have the children not told the truth on occasion? What happened? How did they feel? Did they eventually make things right, and if so, how?

- Have the children ever been wrongly accused of something? What happened? How did they feel?

  Encourage the children to talk about their experiences.

- Talk about the importance of telling the truth. Acknowledge that sometimes it feels like it's hard to tell the truth, but point out that telling a lie often makes things harder later on. Also take the opportunity to point out that it is equally as important for adults to tell the truth as for children.

- Ask children why it is important to admit when they do something wrong and to apologize.

- Look at the end of the story again. Poppy felt much better after she apologized and started to make things right. Why do the children think this made her feel happier?

- Look at the picture story. Ask the children to tell the story in their own words. Why do they think Anna didn't tell the truth right away? Why was Anna's sister mad at her and why didn't she want to play with her?

- Can the children think of specific times when it is especially important to tell the truth? Discuss what can happen when people don't tell the truth.

- Choose children to take the parts of Poppy, Miss Plum, Joe, Lucy, Eva, and Mr. Brown. Invite them to pantomime or role-play the story as you read the text aloud.

Published in North America by Free Spirit Publishing Inc., Minneapolis, Minnesota, 2013.

Library of Congress Cataloging-in-Publication Data
Graves, Sue, 1950–
I didn't do it / Sue Graves ; illustrated by Desideria Guicciardini.
pages cm. — (Our emotions and behavior)
Audience: Age 4 to 8.
ISBN-13: 978-1-57542-445-3
ISBN-10: 1-57542-445-2
1. Truthfulness and falsehood in children—Juvenile literature. I. Guicciardini, Desideria, illustrator. II. Title.
BF723.T8G73 2013
177'.3–dc23
2013012340

Reading Level Grade 1; Interest Level Ages 4–8; Fountas & Pinnell Guided Reading Level I

10 9 8 7 6 5 4 3 2 1
Printed in China
S14100513

Free Spirit Publishing Inc.
Minneapolis, MN
(612) 338-2068
help4kids@freespirit.com
www.freespirit.com

First published in 2013 by Franklin Watts, a division of Hachette Children's Books · London, UK, and Sydney, Australia

Editor: Jackie Hamley
Designer: Peter Scoulding